Life Begins

The Day You Start A Garden

A story based in the tradition of Chinese proverbs

Anthony Johnson

Water Bearer Herbs

Printed in the United States of America
Published by Water Bearer Herbs

ISBN 978-0615885797

Author's Note

As with most manifestations in my life, this story too was unplanned, and is yet another outward expression (albeit one of the more presentable ones) of subconscious and unconscious goings-on. Stuff comes in, gets added to the mental cauldron where it mixes, ferments and is digested before finally being served up in one form or another, all with little effort on my part.

I suppose this story was a sort of gift to me, as a culmination of years of studying and living abroad in Asia, and discovering the incredible world of plants that is our beloved planet Earth.

The Chinese translation of Life Begins the Day You Start a Garden, 人種花命出芽, pronounced "wren jong hua, ming choo ya," is something I created and modeled after the many Chinese proverbs I'd learned while living as a student in Taiwan. I had read the English version of this saying in various locations on the internet, and it was always followed by the description, "An ancient Chinese proverb." Despite that claim, I could never find this Chinese proverb in the Chinese language, which I had hoped to display on a placard in my garden. I performed quite an extensive search, and asked Chinese friends, including scholars, but could find nothing. No one had heard of it.

When explaining my predicament to a close friend one day, he came up with the idea that I create a Chinese version of the proverb myself. It was so simple a suggestion, but one which contained within it a magnificent grandness. Since Chinese proverbs were traditionally born out of fables, this task rebooted my creative side, which had been growing increasingly stagnant. My mental cauldron was back in business! I hope you enjoy this simple yet not-so-simple story as much as I have.

Special thanks to my sister, Nancy,
who always encourages, to my good friend,
Tomohiro, who is a timely source of inspiration,
and to my mother, Clara, for giving us kids
a little bit of her 6th sense.

*L*ong ago, there lived a man who had no one in his life. He had no spouse, no family, and neither friend nor foe. He had no riches, no confidence, and no philosophy or faith. Indeed, you could say he had no life at all. He wondered why he could not be like so many others who seemed to lead joyous and content lives. Or like those who trusted and pursued things, like love, happiness and success.

The man thought, "Don't they know that none of it lasts? I have seen, with my own eyes, good people grow old alone. I have witnessed them be used, abused and discarded. I have watched helplessly as close relatives fell ill and died while still in their prime. "With a wave of his hand and a shake of his head he swore, "I refuse to fall prey to false hope!!"

One day, while on his way to the town marketplace, he was stopped by an old man. The old man said, "I am the sage from the ancient temple up in the mountains. I have come to tell you that your life is about to begin."

The man fixed the old sage with a look of skepticism and replied, "You say my life is about to begin? Ha! What nonsense! I am thirty-eight years old. My life is half done!!"

The old sage continued, "Your real life will soon begin. But, you must first meet me at the ancient temple on top of the great mountain, exactly three months from today, before noon."

Baffled, but somewhat intrigued, the man retorted, "Three months from today? Why that'd be February. It'd be the dead of winter! Are you sure that you do not mean my life will end from exposure to the elements?"

Smiling, the old sage repeated, "You could say that your life as you know it will end. But, without fail, you must meet me at the old temple before noon, exactly three months from today. Soon afterwards, your new life will blossom." With that, the old sage bid the man farewell and disappeared amidst the market throng.

On a cold, breezy morning in February, exactly three months after his peculiar chance encounter with the old sage, the man eagerly arose from bed and prepared himself for the climb up the mountain to the temple. Yes, as suspicious and skeptical as he was of the old sage, the man's curiosity had gotten the best of him. But more than that, deep down inside, so deep he hardly knew it was there, was the desire for the old sage's prediction to come true.

The man hurriedly washed up and pulled on his garments, with an extra layer for protection from the winter's relentless cold. He ate a bowl of gruel and drank a cup of stale broth. Afterwards, he slid his hands into gloves and his feet into thick socks and black boots. With everything in order, he swung open the front door to his home and set out for the temple.

He trekked through fields and thickets, hiked over ridges and hills, and waded across an icy bog before finally beginning the scale up the side of the great mountain. Determined, he elbowed his way past tall dried shrubs and kneed aside fallen branches. Using a stick he'd found, he forged a pathway through all sorts of spindly weeds, gristly grasses, jostling bushes and prickly canopies. He lifted the stick high above his head and brought it down swiftly, splitting an opening in a wall of tangled vines. Alas, through the newly cut gap in the mass of dried vegetation, the man saw a clearing. There was a ginkgo tree that towered over everything else like a parent protecting its young. From it ran a cobbled road worn and crumbling from years of supporting devoted visitors to the temple. He followed it until he arrived at a wooden structure.

"The temple!" he said gleefully.

Slowly, the man made his way to the building. It looked abandoned. In fact, he got the impression that no one had been there in years, even decades, or longer. He wondered to himself, *Am I in the right place?*

First, he circled the outside of the temple. He did not see so much as a groundskeeper, much less an old sage. He decided to venture inside. As most of the doors were missing, and even some of the walls, he easily entered the building. From room to room he searched. The only sounds came from drafts that whistled eerily through the halls and cracks in the walls, and some dusty bronze chimes and ceremonial symbols that the wind teased intermittently.

"This has to be it," he whispered. "I hope I'm not late."

The man was unaware of a very thin stream of smoke that snaked its way through the air, encircling him. Had he noticed it, he might have followed it back to a tiny den that lay inconspicuously just around the corner and found what he was looking for. Alas, the incense was just faint enough for him to mistake its appearance for dust and its smell for the natural scents of the temple's aged wood. Thus, the man walked past the corner and continued down a corridor that ended at large etched wooden doors.

He grabbed the metal handles – the coldness penetrating through his gloves – and pushed. But the doors did not give. He pushed once more, harder, again without success. He tried a different strategy, this time pulling both doors with all his might. The first crack and budge were all that were needed. As if it had been waiting an eternity for an opportunity to get past the unyielding entrance, the wind took advantage of the loosened hinges and flung the doors inward toward the man, carrying leaves, dust, and rays of sunlight with it. Several doves flew from under the doors' eaves, out into

14

a large courtyard and up into the sky where they circled and weaved left and right before flying out of view. The moment the man crossed the threshold to the courtyard, the gong of the temple bells rang out. He walked out into the open space, counting in a whisper the number of steps he took in unison with the bell tolls.

"1 . . .," he counted.

"2 . . . 3 . . .," he continued.

"4 . . . 5 . . . 6 . . .," he spoke in a gentle voice.

"7 . . . 8 . . . 9 . . .," he whispered.

"10 . . . 11 . . .," again in an even fainter whisper.

The ringing stopped when he reached the center of the courtyard.

12 O'clock, he thought.

Nearby, he caught a glimpse of a patch of grass, which, although dry, appeared thickly matted and comfortable. He sat there cross-legged and waited . . ., and waited . . ., and waited. The bells rang one O'clock and two O'clock. The man glanced upward with trepidation at the thick clouds that had begun to gather. The bells chimed three O'clock. He grew increasingly discouraged and disappointed with each passing moment. Finally, when the bells rang four times, the man rose to his feet, trampled across the courtyard, marched down the corridor and stormed out of the temple's main entrance. While heading down the cobbled road toward the great Ginkgo, he felt the sting of droplets of chilly moisture on his face.

"Rain?" he grumbled.

He pushed his way through the gap in the wall of vines he had cut open earlier, and began the descent down the mountain. The sky and the man rumbled and mumbled furiously as he scrambled toward home.

Upon reaching his home, he noticed his clothes were covered in leaves, pods, dried twigs and dead flower heads. Itchy from it all, he quickly removed his garments and changed into a clean set. He went out front and shook the debris from his coat and shirt. He went out back and did the same with his trousers and boots.

After the ordeal at the temple, the man became even more resolved in his dire view of the world. He felt twice as introverted and hopeless as he had before making the trip to the ancient temple.

On a cloudy afternoon in May, three months after his descent from the mountain, who did the man happen upon just outside of the marketplace, but the old sage. Seeing the old man in front of him brought back the anger, disappointment and frustration he had felt three months earlier as if it happened only yesterday.

"You!" the man yelled at the old sage. "You're a fake!"

Startled, the old sage turned in the direction of the loud voice. When he saw the man's face red with ire, and his eyes and lips fuming with rage, the old sage began to push backwards through the crowd.

The man, steadily pursuing the old sage, continued with pointed finger, "You're a phony! A fake! You said my life would begin? Ha! Well, not only has it not begun, but it is worse than it was before!"

The old sage nearly stumbled over pedestrians and carts as he continued to back away from the encroaching man. Finally, he turned and started running. The man followed him, but only in half-earnest.

"Wait! Why are you running? Oh, that's right! Because you're a crook!" he yelled before giving up and turning away from the fleeing old sage.

The man hurriedly bought some millet and spirits, and then headed home, feeling distraught and disgusted.

Later that night, it started to rain. Soon, there was thunder and lightning. He threw himself onto his bed and slept through the long, hard rain that continued throughout the night, and the next day, and the next night, and the next . . .

For days the man kept himself locked indoors. Feeling too let down and unmotivated to get up, he spent most of the day and night in bed. On the morning of the fifth day, he was awakened by a noise that seemed to have come from right outside the rear of his house. He got up and opened the back door to investigate. A blur of black and white darted from the porch, sped down the stairs and came to a stop amongst a patch of greenery. The man stood motionless at the top of the steps, in shock from what lay before his eyes.

Starting from the base of the back porch and fanning outward into the yard was a mysterious lush growth of vegetation. There were green and purple leaved herbs, full shrubs with reddening berries, and flowers of every shape and color. The man shook his head and scratched his scalp. *Am I dreaming?* he thought. A black and white cat watched him from between the branches of a leafy bush. Slowly it slinked over to where the man stood and rubbed its flank up against his calves, purring as it did. Still looking out over the yard, the man bent down and patted the cat's head.

A thought struck him. He quickly ran into the house and out the front door – the cat following behind. Sure enough, he discovered a similar miracle in the front yard. There were plants and flowers everywhere. Hummingbirds and bees busied themselves collecting nectar.

"Could it be . . .?" he exclaimed. "No. It's impossible."

But he knew it was true. All of it must have grown from the seeds and pods he shook from his clothing after he returned from the mountain on that regrettable evening three months earlier.

Utterly mesmerized by the enchanted garden, the man spent the entire morning there with the cat, his first friend. Together they went from plant to plant, smelling and touching each one. He collected some leaves and flower petals from a particularly fragrant herb and took them into the kitchen. With them he made a tea, which boasted a delightfulness like no other tea he had ever enjoyed.

"This is even better than any of the teas sold at the market!" he told the cat. He sat on the front porch steps sipping his tea and teasing the cat throughout the afternoon.

The next day, while he was cleaning the mantle, the man caught a glimpse of a woman as she paused to appreciate the flowers in his yard. The woman smelled a few, and then settled on a stalk copiously covered in fragrant leaves and bunches of small pink florets. She snapped it at the base, brought it up to her nose and took another long whiff, before placing it in her burlap bag. She turned and continued briskly up the road that led to the center of town.

The man poked his head out the front door of his home and watched the woman until she disappeared around a bend. Every morning afterwards, the woman stopped by the man's garden to enjoy the flowers, always plucking one that fit her mood that day and taking it with her. It would become the man's morning ritual to sip a cup of tea made from the garden's harvest and wait for the woman to appear. And she always did, without fail.

One evening, the man went to his backyard and gathered some mushrooms, purple stems and red and green leaves, and with them made a stew. The aroma was so appetizing that as he smelled a large ladleful of the broth, he lost himself in a fantasy of a huge joyous banquet where he was the host and great people from all around came to attend. There were judges and clergymen, actors and politicians, laymen and professionals – wonderful people, all with one thing in common: they'd heard about the man who made hypnotically delicious teas and stews that put the Emperor's chefs to shame, and they wanted to try some.

Just as the man was about to unveil his latest gastronomical masterpiece before the drooling crowd of prestigious onlookers, a loud knock on the front door jolted him out of the daydream and back into the humble reality that surrounded him. In his surprise, he threw his hands up, ladle and all, giving himself a face full of the aromatic stew.

The man looked quickly left and right, like a startled wren. Then he stood still, stew dripping from his chin to the floor, at a loss as to what to do. And no wonder; he hadn't had a visitor in almost a year, when three monks came to collect donations for the poor. To his embarrassment, after seeing how lonely the man was, the monks instead said a half-hour long prayer for his happiness and left him with a bag of cornmeal.

"W-what do you want?" the man barked.

Suddenly, a loud voice on the other side of the door rang out in anticipation, "Hello . . .? Anyone home? Hellooo . . .?"

The man, thinking it might be the monks coming to collect donations again, replied, "I don't have anything to donate. M-maybe next year!"

"Haaa, haaa, haaa!!" the voice bellowed. "I'm not here to collect anything. Well, except maybe some of whatever you got cookin' there! I live down the road near the cedar grove. I'm your neighbor!" he continued.

"N-n-neighbor? I don't have neighbors!" the man replied.

"Sure you do! About three of us altogether! I'm the nearest one to you. Just a 20-minute walk! He, he!"

The man slowly reached out and unfastened the latch on his door. He eased the door open and peered out.

A burly man stood smiling. "Smells good! Hope there's enough for two!" Holding up a bottle of wine, the visitor offered, "Here."

The man and his neighbor ate stew, drank wine, and talked and laughed late into the night.

Thus, in a matter of just two days, the man had made his second friend. There was the cat that chased butterflies in the garden every day. The man appreciated the cat's company, and the cat seemed to appreciate his. Then there was the jolly neighbor who had given him the delicious dandelion wine. Once a week thereafter, the neighbor visited the man. He always brought a tasty dish or beverage and an interesting story or two to share. The man enjoyed the time he spent with his neighbor, and the neighbor seemed to enjoy it as well.

The man realized he felt different. Could it be that he was happy? "Naaah!" he dismissed the notion with a wave of his hand and a shake of his head. No sooner had he done that, did he catch a glimpse of his smiling face reflected on the empty wine bottle. He promptly replaced it with a fitting frown.

*A*t his neighbor's urging – "Come on! You owe it to the people! Ha, ha!" he'd teased – the man decided to try his hand at selling goods at the town flea market. He harvested, dried and packaged three types of teas, featuring his own special garden blend. The following Saturday, he arose even before the jays began their morning chorus. He gathered some fresh cooking herbs from the backyard and bundled them at the stem bases. With a duffle bag stuffed with his teas, cooking herbs and a few utensils heaved over his shoulder, the man began the trip to the town center.

When he arrived at the market, he paid the fee for a vending spot and set up shop. Next, he boiled some water to make tea samples for tasting. That out of the way, the only thing left to do was wait. And wait he did. He waited more patiently than he had ever waited for anything before. Yet no one paid more than a fleeting glance.

To ward off the restlessness he was feeling, the man thought he would prepare a cup of tea for himself. It was then that the miracle occurred. The instant he poured the hot water over his tea blend, the air around him became filled with a mouth-watering aroma. Before he could take so much as a single sip of his own tea, a small crowd formed around his stand, their noses raised and twitching as they sought out the source of the enticing smell. Thus, from the time it took the steaming vapors to rise from the simmering leaves and flowers, the man went from twiddling his thumbs to idle the time away, to not being able to pour tea into the cups in his customers' outstretched hands fast enough.

Every week for several months after that, the man brought goods to sell at the flea market. And every time, the goods sold out within the first couple of hours of opening his stand for business.

One afternoon, when but a handful of herbs was left, the man received a most unexpected visitor. It was the woman who stopped by his garden every morning. And wouldn't you know it, a branch from a plant in his yard was protruding from her burlap bag as she stood there. He watched as her eyes fluttered from tea to herbs to boiling kettle to tea again. The next instant, the man found himself the focus of her inescapable gaze. The woman smiled ever so faintly and said, "Ah! I'm too late. You barely have anything left. There's not enough here to season one bowl of soup."

After a moment of awkward silence, the woman added, "Well, I guess I'll just have to come back next week." As she turned to be on her way, the man finally mustered some nerve.

"Wait!" he called. "I'll have some for you first thing tomorrow morning."

"Tomorrow? But the next market's not for another week," the woman responded as she continued walking away.

"No . . . I, I mean . . .," the man started.

"I'll see you next week," she answered, and was quickly swallowed up by the surrounding crowd.

The following morning, the man loaded up a basket with herbs and teas, and waited for the woman to appear in the distance down the road. He sat in a chair and didn't move until she paused by a patch of violet colored blooms. Within seconds he was at the door, basket of herbs in hand. "Miss!" he called out. "I have your cooking herbs . . . and some tea, if you'd like."

The woman was a bit taken by surprise. "Oh! Aren't you the man from the flea market?" she asked, and looked at the house with the door ajar. "You mean you live here?

"Yes. I tried to tell you yesterday. I see you every morning on your way to town. Quite a coincidence, isn't it?"

"I don't believe in coincidence," she answered. The man blushed. "How much do I owe you?" the woman asked, opening her bag to retrieve her purse.

"Please. It's my pleasure," the man interrupted.

"Oh. I wouldn't think of it," the woman insisted, and placed several coins in the man's hand.

"Thank you," she said.

"Thank you," he replied.

Both the man and the woman found themselves a little flustered with embarrassment as she reached out and accepted the basket of herbs. She took a few steps onto the road. Looking back, she inquired, "The basket . . .?"

"Don't worry about it. I'll see you tomorrow morning?" he half asked, half suggested.

Smiling, she answered, "See you tomorrow."

The man watched her continue up the road and didn't stop until she disappeared around the bend.

*S*ome days later, the man received an invitation to attend the wedding of one of his cousins. This cousin lived nearly two days away by train. Had it not been for the train fare enclosed inside the invitation, the man would have declined. *How can I refuse?* he thought. So, he packed seven days-worth of clothes and other necessities, said goodbye to the cat and set out for the train station.

Unbeknownst to the man, on the day that he arrived at the town where his cousin lived, his own town was beset upon by a severe cold front. Leaves in the man's front and back yards withered and fell off of their branches. Stems dried and became blackened. Of course, the flowers were long gone, leaving not a single petal to be found. In the course of one week, the area around his house was transformed into a barren wasteland. All that was left of the lush botanical growth that had been flourishing just days earlier, was a spattering of dry and broken twigs that jutted up out of the cracked ground like partially unearthed fossils.

Upon returning home from his cousin's wedding, the man nearly walked past his own house. It was practically unrecognizable without the exuberantly colorful garden he had expected to see. He stopped dead in his tracks when he saw the bleakness that now enveloped his home. "What . . .? How . . .? My garden!" he wailed as he dropped his bags on the road where he stood and ran up to the devastation.

He could not believe the sight he beheld. He ran around back and made the same discovery. Gone were the juicy green and purple stalks. No more were the alluring blooms, heavily laden with sweet nectars that the bees and hummingbirds eagerly collected. Not a trace remained of the succulent leaves that grew copiously, and behind which the cat would playfully hide.

"The cat! Where's the cat?" the man wondered aloud. He looked and called for the cat all day, but it did not appear. Finally, the man plopped down on his front porch, exhausted from the trip and distressed from the unfortunate discovery he made upon his return from the wedding.

"Everything's worse than it was before my life changed," he groaned. "At least then I didn't miss or want anything or anyone."

The day ended without a sign of the cat. The man went to bed, hoping he would awaken the next morning to find that it had all been a bad dream.

Not only did the cat not return the next day, the day after, or the next, but even the woman, who had stopped by on her way to town every morning since his garden bloomed, did not appear. Finally, a week passed, as the man had feared, without a knock on the door from the neighbor who brought wine and stories.

Without thinking about where he was going or what he was doing, the man found himself wandering around the town flea market. He managed to buy some cured meat and cornmeal, not because he needed them, but because he felt pressed to appear as though he had a purpose. He went from stall to stall, eyes darting here and there. He did not want to admit it to himself, but he hoped he would run into the old sage. He wanted to find out how to get his new life back.

Alas, he returned home and sat slouched over on his bed. It was at that moment that he realized he was lonely again; that for a brief period – a mere few months – the loneliness that had plagued him for years had disappeared. Now it was back like an old gloomy relative.

He mumbled to himself, "Had it not been for those few months of happiness, I would not have even noticed

how lonely and miserable I had always been. Wait . . .!
Did I just say 'happiness?'" He had.

The more he reflected on the past several months, the
harder he found it to deny that he had been happy. In
fact, he finally had to acknowledge that he wanted more.
He missed the cat and its persistent purring. He missed
the cheerful neighbor and his fascinating tall tales. He
missed the charming woman and her daily visits. He
wanted his garden back. Yes. He wanted to be happy
again!

One evening, the man sat staring at his sour face reflected in an empty wine bottle. Or, was it staring at him? He could not figure out which was the case. But it did not matter anymore, for suddenly there was a more pressing concern. He struck upon the brilliant idea that since it had all started with his trip to the ancient temple, perhaps he had only to make the same journey again to reclaim his life.

"That's it! That has to be it! First thing in the morning I'll return to the temple! Then I'll get my life back!" he rejoiced aloud.

He was so excited that he came close to leaving that instant, but realized it would be foolish to attempt the trip in the pitch blackness of the country night.

The next morning, the man arose from bed so early that not even the earthworms were awake. The truth was that he had gotten little sleep.

As he had done the first time, eight months earlier, he gulped down a bowl of gruel and slipped on his garments and boots. This time, however, he wore fewer than before since it was not the dead of winter. He flung open the front door and began his journey to the mountain for the second time.

*H*is village far behind, the man reached the mountain's base. He had traveled through the same field and across the same bog and through the exact same thicket as he had the first time he visited the ancient temple. Only this time, there was one undeniable difference: there were no hedges to duck under, no thorny branches to maneuver around, and no scratchy shrubs to jump over. In fact, there was barely a sign that anything had ever grown there at all. He realized that the same cold front that had destroyed his garden had also left this once thriving paradise a cold and bleak desert.

Compared to the first trip to the mountaintop, this time he arrived with ease. Strangely, at the spot where the great gingko should have been, there was only a massive tree stump. Upon close inspection, he saw all sorts of engravings in the wood. Carved into the cut surface of the severed trunk, was one message that stood out. It appeared to have been made by two lovers. Underneath the message pronouncing the couple's eternal love was a date. The man looked closely, and then looked again. He rubbed his eyes and looked once more.

"What?" the man choked in disbelief. To his shock, the date, which was etched into the part of the wood that would have been inside of the tree when it was alive, was many years earlier. In fact, it was thirty-nine years ago to be exact! "How can that be?" he gasped. "I must have taken a wrong path along the way."

Slowly he turned his head, taking in the entire view around him. He saw bits and pieces of the cobbled road that lead to the temple. No more than eight months had gone by since he was at that very spot. Not thirty-nine years! He hadn't even been born yet. It was impossible. It was unfathomable. Furthermore, the tree had not been a mere stump, but a full grown and healthy, leafy tree. He was starting to feel dizzy. "Have I finally gone mad?" he muttered under his breath.

Suddenly he sensed a peculiarity in the air. It was as if he was utterly exposed and someone was watching him. The man stood up cautiously and looked around again. "Something's going on here!" he announced as if to let whoever was out there know that he knew they were out there. To make it clear to anyone who might be watching that he would not be deterred, he defiantly and pointedly strode along the barely visible cobbled path up the slope toward the temple.

It was not long before another strange realization hit him. When he first visited the temple almost a year ago, the man had followed the path for a distance of no more than two stones' throws before reaching the temple. This time, however, he had already walked thrice that distance and still he saw no sign of the building. Not only that, but a few paces more and the path came to an abrupt end. He turned in all directions, looking up and down the path, but there was no temple.

"One does not overlook an entire temple that stands alone atop a barren mountain," he told himself. "What is going on? I must be losing my mind!" he mused, thoroughly baffled.

He returned to the tree stump, and then back to where the path ended, all the while scanning the area for the old building. But there was not a building to be found. He took a step off of the last stone in the beaten path when suddenly a flash of movement overhead caught his attention. He raised his gaze upward just in time to spot several doves gliding across the sky. They seemed to have come out of nowhere. After briefly circling and weaving left and right, they disappeared from view as quickly as they had appeared. The man took a few more steps, when the eerily familiar gong of the temple bells rang out.

"This cannot be happening! Where is it coming from? There's no temple!" he exclaimed.

He counted each ring while looking this way and that, trying to determine from where they were originating.

"1 . . .," he counted.

"2 . . . 3 . . .," he continued.

"4 . . . 5 . . . 6 . . .," he whispered.

"7 . . . 8 . . . 9 . . .," again in a whisper.

"10 . . .," . . .

"Wait. . . . That's not me," the man softly proclaimed.

"11 . . .," spoke a gentle voice that was not his own.

"Who's there?" the man mumbled.

"12," said the voice a final time.

The man slowly opened his eyes to find the old sage staring intently at his face. Taken aback by the sudden appearance of the old sage, the man started to lunge forward, only to be quieted by the sage who softly yet strongly placed his right hand upon the man's sternum. The man was enveloped by an indescribable calm.

"Where am I . . .?" His question tapered off while he took in the surroundings: the glistening sound of brass ceremonial symbols and chimes that gently filled the air; the enticing woody incense that drifted dreamily across the room; and the reflection of flames from what looked like a hundred candles that danced across the walls, bounced off of the brass symbols, and landed on the face of the smiling old sage. It all combined to create a most tranquil atmosphere.

"You are at Blue Clouds Temple, the ancient temple of Blue Clouds Mountain," the old sage answered.

"B-b-but I . . . I couldn't find the temple. I looked all over. The tree is gone. All that remains is an old stump. I thought . . . I thought I was lost . . .," the man rambled.

"Here. Sip this," the old sage said as he offered the man a cup of some herbal concoction. "Relax and listen. I have a lot to explain to you," he continued. The man

breathed in the pungent vapors and leaned back.

After some time, the man emerged from the temple and slowly began the trip down the wintry mountainside. In a half daze from the incredible story he had just heard, the man tried hard to understand everything the old sage told him and what it all meant. He recalled the sage's words.

Drink. Forget and remember past and present

Not a dream. Possibilities.

Once again, following the familiar cobbled path, the man came to the huge gingko tree. It was still there after all, its majestic frame adorned with countless fan-shaped leaves that trembled vibrantly in the breeze.

"It is true, then!" he sulked. "It was all a dream!"

Almost in a trance, he continued the descent toward the village, unaware of the cold. He barely even noticed and was utterly unconcerned with the dull pain that began at the sole of his heel. The only thing he was aware of was the echoing in his head of the revelation he had received from the old sage.

Close your eyes and see!

On that day, your life will begin!

*A*t last the man arrived at his home. It was the way it had always been for the past 10 years, just as the old sage had cautioned him it would be. After all, only a few hours had passed since he'd first visited the temple, not several months! Of course there was not even the remotest sign that a garden had ever existed. And why would there be? It hadn't. And it most certainly was not because a severe cold front had destroyed everything.

It simply never was.

Naturally when the man entered his home he found it unchanged. The ladles and pots and pans were still hanging on the walls untouched. The cups were turned upside-down on the countertop, as he had left them early that morning. He headed for the back door, which seemed to beckon him. With the door open, he looked out across the vast span of his yard, and recalled the day in the dream when he opened the door and first discovered the amazing garden that had magically appeared out of nowhere. He remembered the cat, his first friend. He thought about the friendly neighbor, and the intriguing woman who visited the garden.

He stood there, lost in nostalgia for the life he had lived in a dream. But more than just a dream; it felt like a life he had really lived at one time. A previous life . . .?

An unseasonably gentle breeze whisked through nearby treetops and washed over him, clearing his mind. Only then did he become aware of the dull pain at the sole of his right heel.

"Uuugh!" he grunted as he squat down to investigate the source of the pain.

"Must have gotten a pebble in my shoe," he surmised.

The man removed his shoe and attempted to shake out its contents. When that failed, he looked inside and shook it again.

"Eh?" he said, puzzled.

Finally, he noticed that the corner of the insole was slightly bulging upward. Lifting the edge of the material, he found nestled in a groove in the heel of his shoe, a small reddish-brown seed. He furrowed his eyebrows and plucked out the seed from his shoe. Holding it between his thumb and forefinger, the man studied the seed closely. It was as though he believed if only he looked hard enough some answers to the confusion he felt would be revealed.

With a shake of his head, he dismissed the notion that the little seed could possibly contain anything of importance and discarded it on the mantle, not caring where it fell. He snatched a dry cloth that was hanging from a rack in the corner and went over to the basin to wash up. First, he washed his hands. Then he gathered some cold water in his cupped palms and leaned forward, closing his eyes. He splashed the cool contents onto his face. Instantly he heard the old sage's voice with the clarity of the clean water that cascaded over his fingers and dripped from his skin.

> *Drink this: the power, wisdom and hope that spring forth from the earth. With the twelfth toll of the bells, you will forget and you will remember what you once had in a previous life, and what you can have in this one. It is not a dream, but possibilities. Close your eyes and see the promise of the future!*

The man froze for a moment hunched over the basin. He rubbed his face vigorously with both hands, collected another two handfuls of water and splashed it on his face. The old sage's words rang out as vibrantly as the temple bells.

With the twelfth toll of the bells, the twelve

chains of human suffering that bind you will

fall away and you will open your eyes. Now,

take the next step and plant the seed. On

that day, your life will begin.

Your life will begin on the day that you start a garden.

Without having ever thought about what he was doing, the man found himself standing on the back porch with a bowl of water. He descended the stairs and took twelve steps out into the yard. On the twelfth step he stopped, knelt down and placed the bowl on the ground. Using a twig, he made a shallow groove in the frostbitten soil. His hand fiddled about in his shirt pocket until it found what it was looking for.

From the pocket, he produced the reddish-brown seed, which he had earlier tossed onto the mantel. Gently the man set the seed into the groove he had created in the dirt, and covered it with soil. He tamped that down with his fingers and sprinkled some dried leaves, twigs

56

and grass on top of that, which he let remain loose. Finally he scooped up some water from the bowl into his palms and drizzled it over the place where he had planted the seed. He scooped up another palm full of water, and another and another, continuing until the bowl was empty.

When he finished, a small puddle had formed. The man silently watched the shallow pool become smaller and smaller as the water disappeared deep into the earth.

Soon - after the last drops seeped beneath the ground's surface - a faint smile sprouted and grew across the man's face.

The End

About the author

Anthony Johnson was born on the east side of the San Francisco bay area. He graduated with Bachelor of Arts degrees in Japanese and Mandarin Chinese, and has lived in Taiwan and Japan. After returning home to California, he spent many years working as an export manager for a Japanese company, which allowed him to travel around the world. Anthony Johnson resides in Oakland, California, where he works in his garden and practices herbalism.